Never give up.

The
Bogsproggler

Have you ever heard of The Bogsproggler? It's famous round these parts, everyone knows about it. Eight-foot-tall, big red glowing eyes, razor sharp teeth and claws, that can slice through steel like a hot knife through butter. It's even been said it eats children... or so the people of Balen-Town believe.

Balen-Town is a big mining town situated in the heart of Dalanor. Famous for its high-quality iron from the Iron Mountains in the north, and the finest diamonds from the New-Born Mountains in the South. It is said to have the best swords, armour and jewellery in all the land. Hundreds move to the town every year to settle and try and make a living.

Just outside of town to the west are the Black Woods, creeping high up the hill-side as far as the eye can see. Up, up, up they go, to the clearing, then back down again. The woods end and the marshes begin. No one has set foot on these marshes for a hundred years. No man, woman, or child dare walk through the Black Woods.

The story goes that if you walk in the Black Woods and lose sight of Balen-Town through the thick dark trees, The Bogsproggler will get you and you will never be seen again.

In the middle of the marsh sits a cave. The mouth of the cave is open wide like a frog waiting to catch flies, it's dark except for one tiny glimmer of light coming from the back.

Deep in the cave sits a creature sucking on a small rock. No bigger than three feet tall, almost entirely round, with small webbed toes and big wide eyes. This odd creature is... you guessed it, it's a Bogsproggler, not what the people of Balen-Town thought at all. He is also the last of his kind.

Bogsprogglers have lived on these marshes for hundreds of years. They are shy creatures that like nothing more than to sit in their cave and eat. But they don't eat children, not at all, far from it. They like to eat moss. Lots and lots of yummy, green

moss. But the moss in the cave is running out and the Bogsproggler knows this.
"What am I going to do?" The Bogsproggler thinks. Bogsprogglers are very deep thinkers but they cannot speak like you and me. They communicate through odd grumbles and squeaks, but they do understand our language.

"The other cave, now I remember," he squeaks.
At the back of his cave there is a drawing on the wall, drawn long ago by his grandfather. It is very large and crudely drawn with glitter chalk. Glitter chalk was something invented by Bogsprogglers a long time ago. It works just like ordinary chalk, but once a drawing is finished it glows and sparkles in the dark, so it can easily be seen.
The drawing shows directions to another cave filled from wall to wall with all the moss a Bogsproggler could eat.
"But how am I going to get there?"

As I said before, Bogsprogglers are shy, and don't really like being out in the open for too long. The other cave is in the Blue Woods on the other side of Balen-Town. This would mean having to leave his cave, crossing the marsh, going through the Black Woods, up Black Wood Hills and back down into Balen-Town, crossing Balen-Town into the Blue Woods and in to the cave filled with lovely, tasty, green moss.

The sun shines brightly in the sky and lights up the open marshes; the Bogsproggler's cave looking like a grey igloo stuck in the middle. Out of the darkness pops a little webbed foot, then quickly back into the shadows. Slowly out again, this time for a bit longer, and then slowly back in again. Then all of a sudden out pops The Bogsproggler. He looks up to the bright blue sky and squints. It has been a long time since he has been outside his cave, and it takes a while for his eyes to adjust.

"The Black Woods," The Bogsproggler thinks as he looks across the soggy marsh.

The marsh is a big, flat, wet place with the Bogsproggler's cave right in the middle, the Black Woods to the east, marshland as far as the eye can see to the west, Lester Lake to the South and the start of the Iron Mountains to the north. "I best make a move, it will be night in a few hours."

As shy as Bogsprogglers are, they are very playful creatures. As he crosses the marsh he plays a little game with himself, hopping from one rock to another to avoid falling into the swamp. Just as well as the Black Wood Marsh has a reputation for being one of the smelliest in all the land, a mixture of rotten eggs, mouldy fish and smelly old boots. One slip and the little Bogsproggler will smell bad for a week. Yuck!

As the Bogsproggler nears the edge of the woods he sees something dart in-between the trees.
"What was that?" he squeaks. A tall dark figure moves out from behind a tree and then runs off into the woods. *Grumble grumble,* "Must have been a deer."

The air is cooler in The Black Woods; the sun doesn't reach all the way to the forest floor due to the trees being tightly packed together. This is much more bearable for a Bogsproggler; being in the sun to long would dry out his little webbed toes.

Grumble grumble, "It's a long way to Balen-Town from here."

Suddenly, in the corner of his eye he sees what he thought was the deer race between the trees.

SQUEAK SQUEAK! "Wait for me."

Now, Bogsprogglers can't run very fast, as they are not very tall and have very short legs, but that won't stop him finding out what keeps jumping around. So as fast as his little webbed toes can carry him he dashes through the trees after the creature, jumping over logs and almost running straight into a tree. This thing, whatever it is, is fast. Darting left to right and back again, over logs, under branches. The Bogsproggler takes a deep breath and goes as fast as he can...

SQUEEEEEEEEEEEEEAK. Then BAM, he trips on a log and hits the floor with an almighty thud.

As he picks himself up and looks around he sees something very familiar on the ground. A moss-covered pebble. He hops over and sucks the moss clean off. "Yummy."
Just a few feet in front... another pebble. Hop, hop, hop he bounces over to the next one, more tasty moss. The Bogsproggler looks ups and sees a long line of mossy pebbles weaving in and out of the trees. His eyes widen with joy as he hops from one to the next, sucking the moss clean off as he goes.

After a while the pebbles stop. The Bogsproggler looks around and realises that he is lost.
He sees what looks like a big wooden cave in the middle of the woods.
"What? This can't be real" he thinks, "There are no caves in The Black Woods." It's a very strange looking cave. It doesn't have a big, open entrance, just a weird rectangular shape with a small handle on and four large holes covered in glass.

"This isn't a cave, this is a house." *Grumble grumble.*

"And what are you?" a voice says from somewhere between the trees. The Bogsproggler panics and jumps into a bush and hides.
"It's OK little Bogsproggler, I won't hurt you." the voice says. "But you'd better come inside, it's not safe in the Black Woods at night."
The Bogsproggler peers over the top of the bush and sees that the door to the house is open. His eyes are alert looking for where this strange voice is coming from. Slowly but carefully he steps out from behind the bush, still unable to see where the owner of voice is.
"Come on, quickly then!"
The Bogsproggler jumps up and runs into the house and the door slams shut behind him.

The house feels warm and familiar, a large fireplace in the far wall burns brightly. Above the fire a cauldron sits bubbling away. To the right a staircase leads up into the darkness. The Bogsproggler feels at home here, but it is not home; not his home anyhow.

"Hello little one." A voice sounds from the darkness.

Squeak squeak, "Who said that?" cries the Bogsproggler.

"Very rare to see a Bogsproggler round these parts," the voice says.

Grumble "Where is he?" panicked.

"I am here." From the corner, a tall shadow appears, a man steps forward into the room. As he advances, he seems to light up the room.

A tall, thin man with a big white beard dressed from head to toe in green robes looks at The Bogsproggler.

"How are you?" asks the man.

"Me?" squeaks The Bogsproggler.

"Well, you are the one who came through the door, are you not?"

The Bogsproggler stands stunned for a

second, his eyes wide as he lets out a very
soft grumble.
"Can you understand what I'm saying?"
"Well of I course I can," he says with a
smile on his face. "You're speaking Bog."
The Bogsproggler lets out a squeak of joy.
"Wow! I've never met a human who could
understand Bog before."

The tall man lets out an almighty laugh:
"Ho ho ho, nor have I," he says grinning,
and winks at The Bogsproggler.
"Guardians?" The Bogsproggler says
stunned. "You're a Guardian of Black
Wood?"
"You are a clever little fellow, aren't you?"

"He is, isn't he?" Down the staircase comes
another man almost identical to the one
standing in front of the Bogsproggler, he is
dressed from head to toe in blue robes.
Together they stand tall and proud in front
of the Bogsproggler, they look down, eyes
bright, and at the same time they say,
"WE ARE THE GUARDIANS OF
BLACK WOOD, Protectors of The Black
Wood Hills. We swore an oath to the people
of Balen-Town and will continue to guard

these lands for as long as it takes, from the forces of evil that plague these parts."

They look at one another, as if they have been planning to say this to someone for a very long time, they give each other a nod. The one in green takes a step forward. "We have been entrusted to protect these woods and all who pass through it. Long ago we came here as young men. The Brothers of Black Wood they called us."

Still standing with pride in his blue robes the other one says.

"Yes, that's right, I remember. The three Brothers of Black Wood."

"That's correct Brother Blue. Protectors of Balen-Town, sent here many moons ago. I forget how long."

"Brother Green, do you not remember? It's only been one hundred and fifty years"

"One hundred and fifty years! Has it really been that long already? Oh yes... I remember," says Brother Green.

The Bogsproggler, still slightly overwhelmed by the fact that there are now two Guardians stood in front of him lets out a little grumble

"Three brothers?"

Brother Green's face drops and sadness seems to fill the room. "The three Brothers of Black Wood.... I remember now."

"Oh," Brother Blue sighs, "I remember."

Squeak squeak, grumble grumble. "I'm sorry, I didn't mean to say…"

"That's OK little one, you weren't to know," Brother Green says softly.

"Brother Blue, tell our little friend here the story."

The light seems to dim, the fire now just

embers. A strange glow appears around Brother Blue.

"It was long ago, I remember. The three brothers set out from Balen-Town, young, brave... and unprepared for what lie ahead. Brother Green, myself and Brother Red, yes, I remember. Brother Red."

He stands still and looks into the fire place at the fiery embers. He points his finger towards the coals and a spark shoots out of the fire place and seems to dance on the wall.

"Watch and listen, little Bogsproggler."
The glowing spark fills the wall, a moving image appears.

"Not long after setting up here, Brother Red went out one day to look for tasty mushrooms; he was very fond of mushrooms. As the sun started to set Brother Green and myself became aware that he had not returned for his supper, so we set out looking for him." Brother Green clears his throat.

"We had been out for a few hours and it

was now dark. And when it's dark in the Black Wood you do not want to be outside. Luckily, we had our staffs to light the way. Suddenly, we heard an almighty roar and a scream for help. With haste, we ran towards the noise and that's when we saw it."

The house goes dark, and after what seemed like a lifetime a voice said. "The Jackal."

The Bogsproggler stood still, scared stiff. "The Jackal?" he squeaked.

"The Jackal has been around for 200 years. We were sent here to stop it and protect the people of Balen-Town." Brother Blue tilts his head to one side and solemnly says "We failed."

"Now, now Brother Blue, do not be so down, this is not true. We still to this day protect the people of Balen-Town and any who enter The Black Wood."

The Bogsproggler pipes up, "The Blue Woods. that's where I'm heading. I need to cross The Black Woods, up the hill, down into Balen-Town, across the city and into The Blue Woods. The moss in my cave has all run out and my grandfather spoke of another cave near the Blue Wood lake filled with all the moss a Bogsproggler can eat."

Brother Green looks at the Bogsproggler with an odd look on his face.
"You mean to tell us you are going to cross The Black Woods on your own? Ho, ho, ho, well you are a brave little fellow, aren't you?"

The Bogsproggler smiled, then realised that for the first time in a very long time, he didn't feel so lonely. He had been in his cave on Black Wood Marsh for so long all alone, he had forgotten what it was like to talk to someone even if it wasn't another Bogsproggler. *Squeak, grumble, squeak* "Guardians of Black Wood please will you help me get to the Blue Woods so I can find the new cave? This Jackal sounds scary, please help."

"Oh, he is. Eight-foot-tall and razor-sharp teeth, claws that can slice though steel like a hot knife through butter, BIG red glowing eyes and faster than the fastest Guardian," said Brother Blue.

"Brother Blue don't scare our guest."
"But it's true, Brother Green, only being honest."
"This is true, honest is the best way to be. Sorry to scare you little one. We would be honoured to guide you through The Black Woods to Balen-Town."
Squeak "and through the Balen-Town into The Blue Woods and to the cave by the lake?" The Bogsproggler asked, promisingly.

"Unfortunately, little one we can only go as far as the entrance to Balen-Town. One of the great things about being a Guardian is immortality, but this is also a curse as this will only be true if we stay within the area we are tasked with protecting."
Brother Blue walks towards the window and looks out into the darkness. Moonlight dance like fireflies on the trees. He spins round with incredible speed and looks the Bogsproggler straight in the eye.
"Tomorrow we head for Balen-Town!"

The next day they set out for Balen-Town. It is early and the sun beams down between the trees softly illuminating the path. A mist lies on the ground. The Bogsproggler hops along with a big smile on his face chasing the shadows that seemed to bounce off the mist. He had never been this far into The Black Woods before. Following closely behind, the brothers seemed to almost glide, with Brother Green leading the way. The birds sing in unison, a beautiful sad song. Brother Green looks up.
"Ah, the song of the Nin." The Nin is a brightly coloured bird that sits way up high

in the branches, with feathers of bright red, yellow and orange. At dusk, just before the sun sets, if you look high into the tree tops, it almost looks like hundreds of candles burning bright atop a cake.

"Sad yet uplifting at the same time. As long as the bird-song is high in the tree tops of The Black Woods no harm shall come to us on our journey. They guide us to Balen-Town and look over us from above." Brother Green says with hope in his voice.

"Oh, I remember," says Brother Blue.

Grumble squeak, "It's beautiful," says The Bogsproggler as he zips in and out between trees, looking in every nook and cranny he can find for a scrap of moss to nibble on.

"I found some, I found some." He squeaks as he reaches his little hand into a hole in the side of a tree. If he could, he would eat all day every day. Unfortunately, this is what has led to the lack of moss in his cave.

The trio march on together, they still have a long way to go to Balen-Town. Every step they take deeper into the woods the light seems to slowly dim even though it is only midday. After what seems like a very long time, they come to the bottom of a hill. The trees up the hillside are even more tightly packed. A narrow path leads up the side of the hill, as straight as an arrow up into the darkness. The trees seem to arch over the path to form a long, dark tunnel. The Bogsproggler looked up at the menacing trees and gasps. "Wow, that's amazing. Let's go." And without hesitation he starts to run and hop up the path.

After another few hours of hopping and running up this path he reached the top of the hill and came to the clearing in the trees. A small rocky area with tufts of grass dotted around, very much like the outside of his cave, in Black Wood Marsh. The sun was slowly setting in the sky and the Nin bird's song still rang out echoing around the rocks. After a few minutes, the brothers also appeared from the dense woodland. "Stay close little one, we still have to make it down the other side and into Balen-

Town."

Squeak squeak "OK Brother Green"

Suddenly, the brothers freeze stiff.

"Listen," Brother Green said, his voice
trembling.

"What? I don't hear anything," squeaks the
Bogsproggler.

"My point exactly."

Brother Blue scans the tree tops:

"The Nin birds are leaving."

The Bogsproggler looks up to the tree tops:
Hundreds of bright orange, yellow and red
dots, flying off into the distance.

"This can't be good." he grumbles.

The sun slips down behind the trees. Pitch
black and not making a sound, the trio
stand in the darkness. No one says a word,
until…

"Brother Blue, quickly get a fire going."
With ease Brother Blue appears to glide
onto one of the rocks jutting out the
ground, and aims his staff and shouts,
"Lightox." An almighty orange blast shoots
from the end of his staff and ignites the
rock. The flames roar and crackle.

"Quick little one, stay close to the flame,"
Brother Green says. The Bogsproggler

jumps up on the rock and runs up to
Brother Blue, staying close to his side.
They stand in a line next to the fire looking
at the flames. The Bogsproggler looks past
the fire into the woods in the distance.

"What's that?" *Grumble squeak.*

"What?" The brothers say.

"Over there, past those trees." The
Bogsproggler points his little finger at
something glowing in the woods. Glowing
red.

"The Jackal." Brother Green pulls the
Bogsproggler behind him. "Stay behind me
and do exactly as I say!" he snaps.

The red glow gets closer, just as it's about
to show itself, it stops at the tree line. It just
waits there, staring right at the group.

"Don't move. If you turn your back and
take your eyes off it, it will be on top of
you faster than you can imagine." Brother
Blue says. He takes a step forward to the
edge of the rock and points his staff
towards the tree line.

"Boltfly!" A flash of white and blue entwined lightning shoots out towards the woods. With a loud BANG, it strikes a tree, followed by a blinding flash. Once the light dims Brother Blue peers deep into the woods.

Squeak,

"Did you get it?" asks Brother Green.

"I'm not sure," replies Brother Blue softly.

"ROAAAAAAAAAAAAAAAAAAAR," a terrifying shriek rings out.

"I think not." Exclaims Brother Blue *Squeeeeeeeeeeeeek*, "Over there over there." Cries the Bogsproggler.

The Jackal darts from tree to tree, getting closer to the group. Out of the darkness it steps, a hideous creature, eight-foot-tall, thin but muscular and with razor sharp teeth, its mouth drooling and snarling as it breathes menacingly. Its arms raised high up above its head, claws six inches long at the end of each finger pointing ready for attack.

"What do we do?" *Grumble grumble*. The Jackal races towards them with incredible speed. Brother Green kneels and quickly shouts "Obstructor!" A green shield

25

suddenly appears around the Bogsproggler and the brothers. The Jackal starts slashing and hitting at the protective barrier with all its strength. It roars and lets out a blood curdling scream.

Brother Blue turns to The Bogsproggler. "Quick, little one come here! This barrier won't hold for long."

"QUICKLY" shouts Brother Green, "it's getting through, I can't hold it much longer!"

Scared, but also a little excited by all the commotion he hops over to Brother Blue. "Take this, little one," says Brother Blue. He gives the Bogsproggler a small bottle. *Squeak, grumble* "What is it?"

"It's a potion we have been working on for the last sixty years. It will give you invisibility for a short time. But use it wisely! It only has enough for three uses." *Grumble, squeak* "What about you? why don't we all use it and make a run for Balen-Town?" *Grumble.*

"We can't. We still haven't perfected it for us. Everything else we have tried it on seems to go invisible but not us, hmm, never been tested on a Bogsproggler mind you. Quick, drink up!"

"BROTHER BLUE! HELP!" shouts Brother Green. "The shield is dropping." Brother Blue swiftly points his staff and shouts "Obstructor!" A blue shield joins the green one. The two blend together and light up the sky a beautiful turquoise.

The Jackal stops his attack and jumps back, growling at the brothers. The Bogsproggler, transfixed by the amazing light show, almost forgets where he is. Brother Green shouts to him, "Little one, listen up!" The Bogsproggler appears a little confused for a second then looks at Brother Green.

"The potion, quickly, drink it."

He looks at the bottle and takes a sip. It tastes sweet and he licks his lips.

"One more thing little one... take this." Brother Green hands him a small bracelet "What is this?" he says as he sniffs and tries to eat it.

"Don't eat that, it's a bracelet of speech. Wear it and you will be able to speak and understand any language. The people of Balen-Town don't take kindly to the unknown. A Bogsproggler hasn't set foot in Balen-Town... well, ever. Stay out of sight and cross the city. However, if you do get caught you may need to talk your way out. Now, GO, make haste!"

"Go? Go where?"
The Jackal steps back slowly and seems uninterested for a split second before moving round and attacking from another angle. Its claws slightly tear the shield. Brother Blue lets out a cry. "Quickly little one, head down the hill to Balen-Town. We will protect you."

Squeak, grumble, squeak, "No. we have to stick together!" At that point, the potion begins to work and the Bogsproggler starts to fade away. "What's happening?"
"It's working! Now, run for Balen-Town! Don't look behind you and don't stop for anything!"
The Jackal swipes at the shield relentlessly, each strike hitting harder and harder.
With a combination of fear and excitement in his eyes the Bogsproggler fades away

completely.

Just as he is about to leave the shield, The Jackal strikes the top of Brother Green's staff, shattering it into hundreds of tiny wooden splinters. The protective shield changes from turquoise to blue and its power halves. The Jackal lets out a howl that pierces the darkness and his eyes glow a bright red as he attacks again.

"Run little one! Run as fast as you can!" yells Brother Green.

The Bogsproggler, now completely invisible, jumps down off the rock out of the safety of the shield and runs across the plain to the hillside. Down through the thick woods he can see the fires of Balen-Town burning bright. He turns to see the Brothers still in the shield just managing to hold off the attack from The Jackal. He knows he can't help and lets out a small, sad, squeak.... "I'm sorry."

He turns and runs down the hill as fast as he can.

The Brothers know the shield's power won't last very long against the Jackal, and wait for the perfect time to launch a counter attack.

Brother Green hurries to fix his staff.

 "Brother Blue, when I say, release the shield and get ready."

The Jackal seems to tire and slows his attack down.

"NOW!" shouts Brother Green.

Brother Blue releases the shield, and as he does so Brother Green stands tall behind him and shouts with an almighty boom "Boltfly!" followed by Brother Blue, "Lightox!"

Flashes of white and blue electricity, combine with yellow and orange fire to form a massive orb that shoots from the end of their staffs so incredibly powerfully it appears to fill the sky. It hits The Jackal sending it flying back into a tree.

It tries to stand but falls and slumps against the tree.

"Did we get it brother?"

"I think we may have Brother Blue."

Brother Blue squints in the darkness and sees no movement from the beast.
"The Jackal of Black Wood. We did it Brother Red, you can rest in peace."
Brother Blue says with a smile on his face.

"Oh yes, now I remember. Brother Red, go in peace." Follows Brother Green
The glow in The Jackal's eyes fades away, its lifeless body slips to the floor. The Brothers stand upon the rock next to the fire. They relax and look into the forest with happiness in their hearts. They turn and smile at one another, and. When suddenly, out of the darkness a pair of red glowing eyes appear, and then another, and another.

On the edge of the wood, a shallow river runs alongside the towering wooden walls of Balen-Town. Thick, strong oak protects all inside from unwanted guests, thieves, and creatures of the night. A low but wide bridge made of cobblestones crosses the river and leads up to an intimidatingly large iron gate sealed shut. Two guards armed with swords and shields talk and laugh as they keep warm by the fire, while also keeping a watchful eye on the road. A young boy no older than eleven or twelve sits on the edge of the bridge, his legs dangling over the edge as he chucks pebbles into the water and watches the ripples. He is dressed in worn-looking clothes, and his boots are tatty.

"You there, boy!" bellows the guard, "Best be in, night is here, come on." He turns back to his friend and they continue to talk. The boy looks up solemnly. He stands up, dusts himself off and turns towards the gate. Just as he's about to leave, he catches a glimpse of something small dashing through the woods towards the river. When suddenly... SPLASH! Out of the woods comes The Bogsproggler, tumbling over a rock and falling face first into the river.

"Ow, my face!" he thinks as he picks himself up. He shakes his head and looks around "Wow, MOSS!" he squeaks. Sure enough, the very rock he took a tumble over is covered in yummy, green, fresh moss. The Bogsproggler squats down and starts to nibble away, as if he has completely forgotten the reason he was running out of the woods. Bogsprogglers tend to have a habit of doing this, but soon enough he remembers and stands up, looking into the forest to check that he hasn't been followed.

"Hello!"
The Bogsproggler freezes. "Who or what was that?" he thinks.
"What are you? You're a funny looking thing," the voice says.
Without turning around, The Bogsproggler jumps back over the rock and into the tree line without hesitation.
"It's OK, I won't hurt you." The boy from the bridge stands on the bank opposite the woods. He extends his hand and beckons to The Bogsproggler. "Come on, it's OK."
From behind the rock a small pair of eyes appear, wide and scared, his little hands

resting on the rock.

"You like moss?" the boy says, smiling. "Well look how much moss is here!" He points to the bank's edge. The Bogsproggler's eyes light up and he jumps up from behind the rock.

"MOSS!" he shouts uncontrollably, then dashes across the river to the other side and starts eating away.

"See, it's tasty," the boy says as he looks at the Bogsproggler with a bewildered expression on his face. "Oh, you brought a friend." He points into the woods.

The Bogsproggler turns around and in the woods, a big pair of red glowing eyes approaches slowly.

Jumping out of the water and onto the bank with the boy, the Bogsproggler shouts, "We need to get inside!" The young boy's face changes from intrigue to fear.

"Quick this way!" He jumps into the river and down towards the bridge. Knowing that the guards would not allow his new friend into Balen-Town due to its *humans only* policy. He heads towards an iron grate under the bridge. He pulls open the grate. "Jump in, this is my secret way in and out." As quick as mice they jump in and with an almighty crash the grate slams shut behind them. They continue to run down a small sewer network deep underground and finally come to a stop.

"We're safe here," the boy says, panting as he looks at his new, odd-looking friend.
"Here? Where is here?" the Bogsproggler grumbles nervously.
The boy catches his breath, looks the Bogsproggler in the eye and says.
"Welcome to Balen-Town."

To Be Continued

Printed in Great Britain
by Amazon